MW00831728

Clown's Pants

Written by Jill Eggleton
Illustrated by Craig Smith

Clown looked
at his pants.
"Yuck!" he said.

Clown washed his pants.

He put his pants
on the fence.

The wind came . . .
whooo-ooo-ooosh!

whooo-ooo

Clown's pants went away.
They went up, up
into the sky.

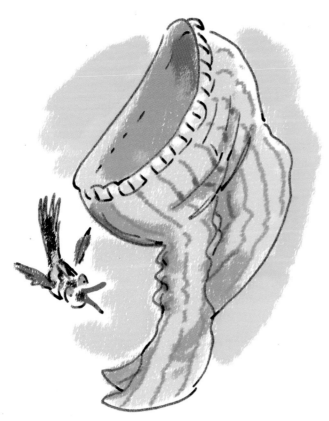

The pants went
over the sea.

"**Look!**" shouted
the people
on a boat.
"A big kite!"

The pants went
over the mountains.

"**Look!**" shouted
the people
on the mountain.
"A big bird."

The pants came down
in the jungle.
A monkey saw
the pants.
He put the pants on.

Clown went
to get his pants.

"My pants are
not here!" he said.

"Where are my pants?"
said Clown.

On a monkey!
On a monkey!

Advertisement

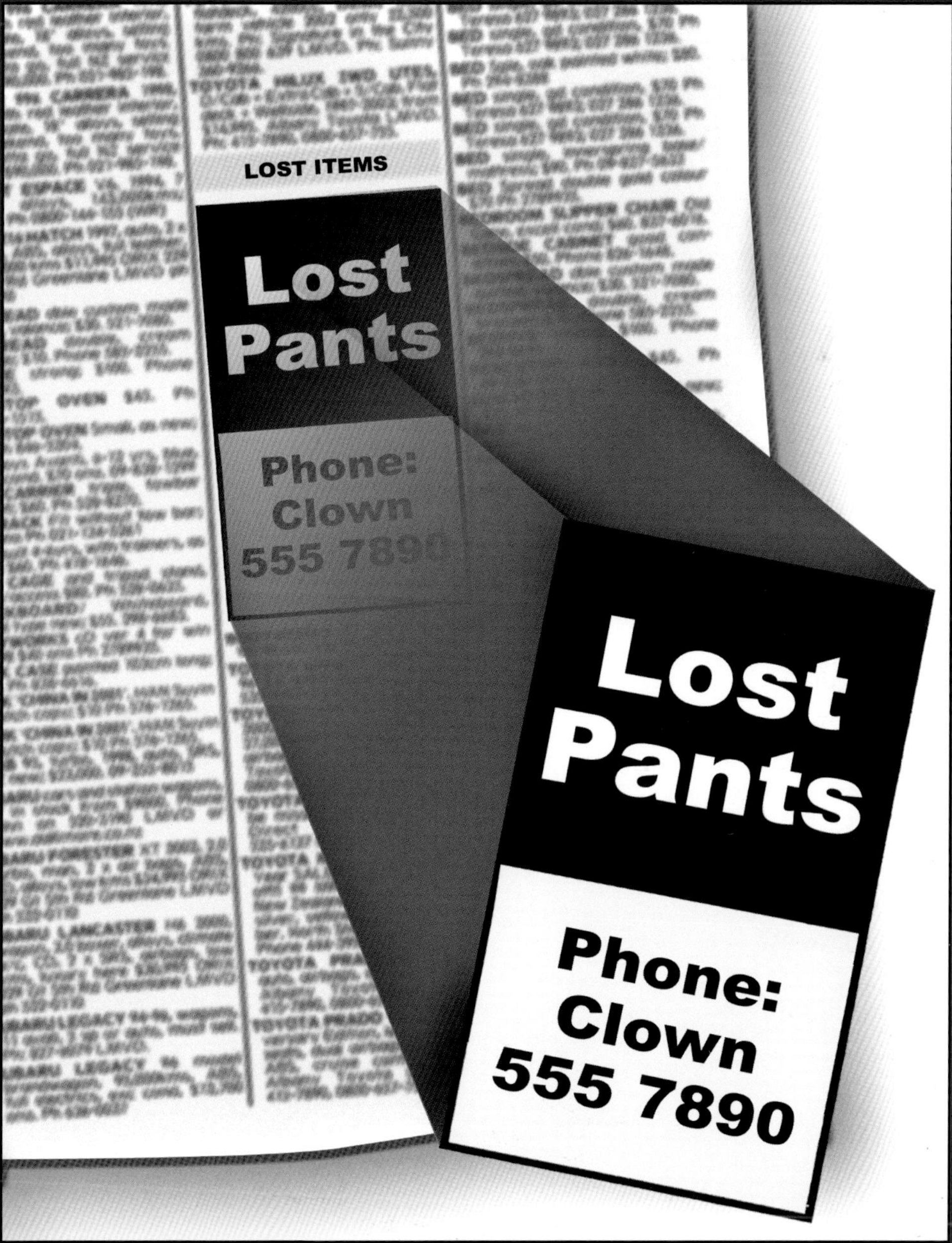

Guide Notes

Title: Clown's Pants

Stage: Early (2) – Yellow

Genre: Fiction

Approach: Guided Reading

Processes: Thinking Critically, Exploring Language, Processing Information

Written and Visual Focus: Advertisement, Speech Bubble

Word Count: 108

THINKING CRITICALLY
(sample questions)
- What do you think this story could be about?
- Focus on the title and discuss.
- Why do you think the people thought Clown's pants were a big kite?
- Why do you think the pants came down?
- What do you think made the monkey put the pants on?
- How do you think Clown might get his pants back?

EXPLORING LANGUAGE

Terminology
Title, cover, illustrations, author, illustrator

Vocabulary
Interest words: pants, fence, kite, boat, mountain, jungle, monkey, whooosh, people
High-frequency words: saw, his, get, away, came
Positional words: on, up, into, over, down, in

Print Conventions
Capital letter for sentence beginnings and names (**C**lown), periods, commas, quotation marks, exclamation marks, question mark, ellipsis